The Angry Elf

Pixie Tricks

Read All the Magical Adventures!

Pixie Tricks

The Angry Elf

Written by
Tracey West

Illustrated by
Xavier Bonet

BRANCHES™

SCHOLASTIC INC.

In memory of my friends Dan and John,
two angry elves with hearts of gold. —TW

For my children, Daniel and Marti.
You're pure magic. —XB

Text copyright © 2000, 2022 by Tracey West
Illustrations copyright © 2022 by Xavier Bonet

Library of Congress Cataloging-in-Publication Data

Names: West, Tracey, 1965–author. | Bonet, Xavier, illustrator.
Title: The angry elf / written by Tracey West; illustrated by Xavier Bonet.
Description: New York, NY: Branches/Scholastic Inc., 2022. | Series: Pixie tricks; 5 |
Summary: Violet and her fairy friend Sprite hatch a plan to catch Fixit, a toy-making elf whose lack of appreciation drives him to break all the toys he creates, but pixies Rusella and Spoiler are determined to thwart Violet and Sprite's plans.
Identifiers: LCCN 2021002549 (print) | ISBN 9781338627909 (paperback) | ISBN 9781338627916 (library binding)
Subjects: CYAC: Fairies—Fiction. | Pixies—Fiction. | Friendship—Fiction.
Classification: LCC PZ7.W51937 An 2022 (print) | LCC PZ7.W51937 (ebook) | DDC [Fic]—dc23
LC record available at https://lccn.loc.gov/2021002549

10 9 8 7 6 5 4 3 2 1   22 23 24 25 26

Printed in China   62
This edition first printing, March 2022
Book design by Sarah Dvojack

Table of Contents

Whenever pixies do escape
Through the old oak tree,
Here is what you have to do
Or trouble there will be.
First find a Pixie Tricker,
The youngest in the land.
Send him to the human world,
The Book of Tricks in hand.
Once he's there, he'll find a girl
Who's only eight years old.
But she's a smart and clever girl
Who's also very bold.
He must ask her for her help,
And if she does agree,
They'll trick the pixies one by one
Till no more do they see.
Only they can do the job.
It's much more than a game.
For if they fail to trick them all,
The world won't be the same!

1
A Party

"What pixie should we look for today?" Violet Briggs asked.

"Yeah, I'm ready for some pixie-tricking action!" her cousin Leon added as they walked home from school.

A tiny fairy with yellow hair and pale green skin popped out of Violet's backpack. He fluttered his shimmery rainbow wings.

"I'm not sure," Sprite replied. "There hasn't been a sign of a new pixie in days."

Violet's life had changed so much since the day she met Sprite. He had come through a magical door in the oak tree in her backyard.

Sprite had explained that fourteen pixies had escaped from his world. It was Sprite's job to trick them and send them back. And the fairy queen said he needed an eight-year-old girl to help him.

Violet had agreed to help, and Leon had joined them. Since then, they had tricked five pixies together.

"Maybe we could look in the park today, and then over by the library tomorrow," Leon suggested.

Violet shook her head. "We can't look for pixies tomorrow. It's Brittany's birthday party, remember?"

Leon scratched his head. "Is it tomorrow? I thought it was next week."

Violet took the party invitation out of her backpack. "No. This says Wednesday."

Sprite fluttered up to Violet's face. "A party? Can I go?"

Violet frowned. "I'm not sure that's a good idea, Sprite. Brittany is my best friend, but I can't tell her about you. She'd put you on the front page of the school newspaper!"

"I'll stay hidden!" Sprite promised. "Please!"

"I'll think about it," Violet said. They had reached the yellow house where she and Leon lived. "Let me go inside and get my pixie-tricking tools."

Violet left Leon and Sprite outside. She ran up to the second floor. Her dad was strumming on his guitar. Today was his day off from the restaurant where he worked with Violet's mom. He smiled at Violet.

"Hey there. How was your day?" he asked.

Before Violet could answer, her dad's phone rang.

"Hi! She's right here," he said. Then he handed the phone to Violet. "It's Brittany's mom. Brittany wants to talk to you."

Violet heard her friend's voice on the other end. "Violet, did you and Leon forget? You're supposed to be at my party!"

2
The Wrong Day!

"What do you mean?" Violet asked her friend. "I thought your party was tomorrow."

"No, it's today," Brittany told her. "I've been talking about the party all day."

"Yeah, but I thought you were just excited for *tomorrow*," Violet explained.

Brittany sighed. "Everyone was supposed to come right after school. It says so right on the invitation."

Violet took out the invitation again. She blinked. Now the invitation said Tuesday.

But I was sure *it said Wednesday!* she thought. *That's weird!*

"Brittany, I'm so sorry," Violet said. "We'll get there right away."

Violet hung up and spun around. "Dad! Brittany's birthday party is right now! I got the date totally mixed up. Can you drive me and Leon to her house?"

Her dad strummed the guitar. "*You got it!*" he sang.

Violet thought fast. She ran outside and told Leon about the mistake. Then she went back inside and found her present for Brittany. She scrambled around the kitchen, looking for the wrapping paper, scissors, and tape.

Leon came into the kitchen, carrying his present in a gift bag. His eyes lit up. "Is that a Dancing Dolphin Waterfall?"

Violet nodded as she wrapped the gift. "Yes! When you press a button, it lights up and the waterfall turns on. Then dolphins dance up and down. Brittany is going to love it!"

Mr. Briggs joined them. "Are you two ready to go?"

Violet stuck a bow on the box. "Yup!"

They hurried outside, and Violet and Leon got into the back seat of the Briggs' car. As Violet's dad started the engine, she remembered something.

"Wait, where's Sprite?" she whispered to Leon.

Sprite poked his head out of Violet's hoodie pocket. "Right here! I can't wait for the party!"

3
Toy Trouble

"Violet and Leon, you made it!" Brittany said happily as she opened the door. The words BIRTHDAY GIRL glittered on her shirt. She wore her black hair in a long braid.

"Sorry about the mix-up," Violet said.

"It's okay. We're about to open presents!" Brittany replied. She led Violet and Leon to the living room. Orange balloons and streamers hung everywhere. Orange was Brittany's favorite color.

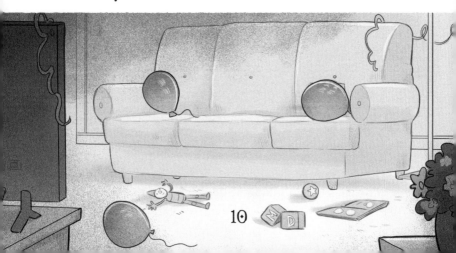

10

All of Brittany's closest friends had come to the party. Leon sat next to his friend Evan on the floor. Violet put her gift on a pile of presents and found a seat next to Lila and Anna.

Violet gently tapped her hoodie pocket, and felt Sprite safely curled up inside.

Brittany sat in a chair near her presents.

Her little sister, Ruby, clapped her hands. "Open your presents! Open your presents!" she chanted.

Brittany picked up a box wrapped in pink paper.

"That's from me," Anna said.

Brittany opened the present. She took out a purple music box. On top stood a tiny ballerina.

"Oh, it's so pretty!" Brittany said. She turned the gold key on the side of the box. Everyone waited to hear what tune it would play.

Mooooooo! was the noise that came out of the box. *Moooooo!*

Ruby giggled, but Anna blushed. "It's supposed to play 'Dance of the Sugar Plum Fairy.'"

Brittany tried to smile. "That's okay. I, uh, I like cows."

"Open mine next," Leon said. He handed Brittany his gift bag.

Brittany pulled out a box with a round furry creature inside. The toy had big wiggly eyes.

"It's a Fuzzy Pet," Leon explained.

"I know!" Brittany said, tearing open the box. "They're so cute! They talk to you and everything."

Brittany took out the Fuzzy Pet and pressed the button on its belly.

"Hi, I'm your Fuzzy Pet," said the toy.

Brittany smiled. But then—

13

"Scramble the bananas in the pencil patch!" the pet said.

Everyone gasped.

"What did you say?" Brittany asked. She pressed the button again.

"Rumble with the mustard!" the Fuzzy Pet squawked.

Brittany stared at the toy.

Leon scratched his head. "Brittany, this is weird!" he said. "There must be something wrong with that Fuzzy Pet."

"It's all right," Brittany said. But she didn't sound like she meant it.

Violet was worried. Something strange was going on. She could feel it.

Brittany opened the rest of her presents.

She got a sticker set. But none of the stickers were sticky!

She got a stuffed tiger. But it had a tiger's head and a duck's body!

She got a model of the solar system. But the sun was smaller than the planets!

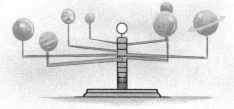

Brittany tried to smile each time. But everyone knew she was disappointed.

Finally, Brittany picked up Violet's gift.

Violet held her breath. *I really hope there's nothing wrong with the Dancing Dolphin Waterfall!* she thought.

Brittany unwrapped the gift. "Oh, Violet, this is just what I wanted!" she said. "We have to try it out."

"Okay," Violet said nervously.

Brittany got a cup of water from the kitchen and poured it into the back of the waterfall.

The kids gathered around the toy. Brittany pushed the button.

Splash! Jets of cold water shot out of the toy. The water sprayed all over Brittany!

Brittany couldn't take it anymore.

"That's it!" she moaned. "This is the worst birthday party ever!"

"Brittany, I'm so sorry!" Violet cried. She ran to get a towel for her friend.

Then she felt Sprite land on her shoulder.

"Don't feel bad, Violet," he said. "I think a fairy is behind all of this!"

4
Fixit

Violet wanted to talk more to Sprite, but she worried someone might see them. She helped Brittany dry off, and tried to cheer her up. Then they all ate pizza and cake and played games until it was time to leave.

When they got home, Violet, Leon, and Sprite met in Leon's room.

"All right," Violet said. "Sprite, do you really think a fairy ruined all of Brittany's toys?"

"Yes," Sprite replied. "I think an elf named Fixit is to blame."

Violet frowned. "An elf? Aren't elves supposed to be *good* at making toys?"

"They are," Sprite said. "But Fixit makes toys that don't work the right way. He doesn't break them. He just fixes them to make them do something different—or awful."

"Why does he do that?" Leon asked.

There was a puff of light, and a pixie appeared in the room. Violet, Sprite, and Leon jumped.

"I do it because kids don't care about all of my hard work!" the fairy said.

He was an elf, about as tall as Violet's knee. He had a white beard and a frowny face. He wore a red cap on his head and buckled shoes on his feet. A tiny hammer hung from his belt.

"Fixit!" Sprite cried. "Why are you here?"

"I heard you talking about me," Fixit said. "It's time people know. I'm tired of working day and night to make toys. What happens? You kids play with them once and throw them away. It's terrible!"

"That's not true at all!" Violet said. "Not everyone treats their toys that way."

Fixit looked around Leon's room. His toys were all over the place.

"Look at this mess!" Fixit said. He glared at Leon. "Is this *your* room?"

Leon nodded, too afraid to speak.

21

"Is this the thanks I get for making toys?" Fixit asked. "You don't even care about them."

Fixit raised the hammer. He pointed it at a toy robot on the floor.

"Fixit Tixif!" Fixit yelled. Lightning bolts flew out of the hammer. They hit the robot.

The robot sat down on the floor. It stuck one thumb into its metal mouth.

"Waaah!" cried the robot. "I want my mommy!"

"That's much better!" Fixit said. "And now I've got to go. I've got more toys to fix!"

Before they could say or do anything, Fixit vanished.

Leon picked up the robot.

"Time to change my diaper," said the toy.

"Oh no," Leon said. "We've got to do something about that elf!"

Then Violet's dad yelled down the stairs, "Bedtime, kids!"

Violet sighed. "We can figure this out tomorrow!"

5
Applesauce Stew

The next morning, Violet woke up early and opened her dresser drawer. Inside, Sprite was curled up in a soft pair of socks.

"Wake up, Sprite!" Violet said. "We need to look in *The Book of Tricks* before we go to school!"

Queen Mab, the fairy queen, had given Sprite the special book. It told how to trick all the escaped pixies.

Sprite took the book out of his bag and turned the pages. "Here's Fixit's page," he said.

There was a blank space where Fixit's picture should be. His picture would only appear once he was caught. Sprite read the poem out loud.

Fixit the elf is angry and snappy.

To trick him,

you must make him happy.

Sprite's wings fluttered. "That can't be too hard!" he said, excited. "We could tell him a joke. Or..."

"We can figure it out together after school," Violet said.

On the walk to school, Violet and Sprite told Leon what they'd learned.

When they got to class, Violet slipped Sprite into her desk.

"Please pass up your science homework," said their teacher, Ms. Rose.

Violet took her homework out of her backpack. Then she froze.

She had done math homework, not science homework.

Other kids looked worried, too. No one passed up their papers.

"What's the matter, class?" Ms. Rose asked.

Brittany raised her hand. "Ms. Rose, I did math homework."

"Me, too!" other kids joined in.

Ms. Rose shook her head. "What an odd mix-up," she said. "You can do the science homework tonight."

Violet sighed, relieved. *At least I'm not the only one*, she thought. *But that sure is strange.*

The rest of the morning went smoothly. When the lunch bell rang, Violet put Sprite in her hoodie pocket.

"Thank goodness," Sprite whispered. "I'm hungry."

But when Violet and Leon got to the lunchroom, something was wrong. Two of the cafeteria workers were arguing.

"I said to put *tomato* sauce in that stew!" one woman said. "Not applesauce!"

"Your message said applesauce!" said the other woman.

"But I didn't—" the lunch ladies stopped when they noticed the students.

The first woman spoke. "You're in for a special treat today, kids!" she said, trying to smile. "Applesauce stew!"

Violet looked at Leon. *Applesauce stew?*

Violet got her lunch and sat down with Brittany and Anna. She picked at the cold, mushy mess in her bowl.

Over at the next table, Evan was showing off his new mini car to Leon.

"This one's a sports car," he said, holding onto the car as he rolled it across the table.

Suddenly, the car shot free from Evan's hand! It jumped up. It slammed into Evan's milk and knocked it over.

"Cool!" Leon said. "It's got a real motor?!"

Evan shook his head. "No, it doesn't. This shouldn't be happening!"

The car zoomed across the table. It crashed into a bowl of applesauce stew, sending it flying off the table. Then it kept going, slamming into every bowl of stew in its path!

"Fixit must've *fixed* Evan's car!" Violet said under her breath.

Violet saw her pocket wiggle. She knew Sprite wanted to know what was happening.

"Violet, look out!" Brittany cried.

Violet looked up. The car zoomed through the air and landed right in her bowl of stew!

Splash! The soggy stew splashed all over Violet's shirt. She grabbed the tiny car before it could take off again.

"Got it!" Violet yelled.

The kids in the lunchroom cheered. Violet handed Evan the car.

"I guess it's broken," Evan said.

Violet didn't answer. She knew the truth. It was all because of Fixit!

She walked over to Leon. "That does it," she whispered. "We've got to find Fixit before he ruins every toy in town!"

6
Fairy Bait

After school, Violet changed into a clean shirt. Then the three Pixie Trickers met in Violet's room.

"Sprite, we need to trick Fixit, fast!" she cried.

Sprite flew up to her face. "You are as angry as that elf!" he said.

Violet tried to calm down. Being angry was no fun.

"To trick Fixit, we have to make him happy," she said. "But I have no idea how to do that, so I think we need to find out more about him first."

"Good idea," Leon said. "Uh, how do we do that?"

"I think we should find him and talk to him," Violet said. "He seemed to like talking to us."

"You mean *complaining*," Sprite said. "But you're right. We should find him."

"Where do you think he is?" Leon asked.

Violet thought. "He's a toymaker, right? Maybe he's at the toy store in town!"

"Great!" Sprite said. He reached into his magic bag for some pixie dust. "We can go there now!"

Violet looked at the clock. "It's almost time for dinner," she said. "We can't go running around now."

Sprite landed on Violet's bed. Nobody talked for a little while.

Then Sprite sprang up. "I've got it!" he said. "We can bring Fixit to us!"

Sprite took out *The Book of Tricks*. He thumbed through the pages.

"Here it is!" Sprite said finally. "A fairy lure!"

"What's a lure?" Leon asked.

"It's like . . . bait," Sprite answered. "Like you would use to catch a fish."

Sprite gave the book to Violet. She took a small magnifying glass from her bag of pixie-tricking tools. Then she looked at the page.

"They're musical notes," Violet said. "I thought you said it was a fairy lure."

"It is," Sprite said. "Pixies love music. We just play the notes on a flute. Then the pixie is lured right to us."

Sprite paused. "You have a flute, don't you?"

Violet went to her closet. "I have this," she said. She took out a recorder, a kind of short plastic flute. "We play it in school."

"That'll do!" Sprite said. "Now play! Play!" Excited, he flew in circles.

Violet studied the musical notes. She thought she knew how to play them.

Violet put the recorder to her lips. She put her fingers over the holes. And she blew.

Sprite covered his ears with his hands. "Maybe you should try again," he said.

"No, please don't!" Leon teased.

Violet frowned. "I just need practice."

She played the notes one at a time, slowly.

Sprite took his hands from his ears. "Not bad," he said. "Play it again."

Violet played the tune again, a little faster. This time it sounded kind of pretty.

"Again!" Sprite said. He did a little dance in the air.

Violet played the tune again.

Just as she played the last note, a fairy appeared.

It wasn't Fixit!

Violet stopped playing. They all stared at the fairy.

She was twice as tall as Sprite. Her dark hair was pulled into a ponytail. She wore a blue sparkly dress.

The fairy folded her arms and stared at Violet and Leon.

"So," she said. "What do you want?"

Violet didn't know what to say. *I was expecting Fixit. Who is this fairy?*

7

Rusella

The fairy tapped her foot on the floor. "Why did you make me come all the way over here?" she asked. "I've got work to do."

Violet found her voice. "Who are you?" she asked.

The fairy rolled her eyes. "You don't even know? My name is Rusella," she said. "And now I've got to get back to work. I'm busy—"

"Rusella!" Sprite cried. "I know about you. You're a message gremlin."

"That's right," Rusella said.

"What's a message gremlin?" Leon asked.

Sprite darted around the room, excited. "Message gremlins like to mix up messages people send to one another," he explained. "Like when you think you're supposed to meet your friend in the park, but your friend is waiting for you at her house."

Violet turned to Rusella. "You've been causing all the trouble around here! You changed the date on our invitations from Brittany!"

Rusella giggled. "And at the last second I changed them back. No evidence!"

"Hey!" Leon yelled. "Did you mess with the cafeteria worker's message? Is that why we ended up with applesauce stew?"

Rusella smiled. "That was a good one, wasn't it? But you haven't seen anything yet."

"What are you up to, Rusella?" Sprite asked.

Rusella got a dreamy look in her eyes. "There are so many messages I can mess up in this town. Text messages. Email messages. Letters that come in the mail. Homework assignments. Everyone will fight and yell at one another. It's going to be great!"

Rusella looked into Violet's eyes. "And after I'm through with this town, I'm going to mess up the whole human world!"

"Sprite, quick!" Violet yelled. "Look in *The Book of Tricks*! We have to trick her!"

Rusella frowned. "Trick me? Sorry. That's not going to happen."

The gremlin took some pixie dust out of her pocket. She sprinkled it on her head.

Then *poof*! She vanished.

"No!" Violet cried.

Sprite read *The Book of Tricks*. "It's okay, Violet," he said. "We wouldn't have been able to trick her anyway. See—here." He read the rhyme aloud.

R usella's mixed-up messages
Are annoying for sure.
A bowl of alphabet soup
Is the only real cure!

"How are we supposed to get her to eat alphabet soup?" Violet asked.

Leon rubbed his stomach. "Mmm, soup. I'm hungry! I couldn't eat any of that gross lunch."

"Lunch!" Sprite cried. "Yes, that's it!" He flipped through the pages of *The Book of Tricks*. Finally, he smiled.

"It's right here! I knew it!" Sprite said. He looked up from the book. "There are lots of silly rules that all pixies have to obey."

"You mean there's a rule about lunch?" Violet asked.

"Not exactly," Sprite said. "But a fairy can't turn down an invitation to a meal. We could invite Rusella to lunch . . ."

"And serve her alphabet soup!" Violet chimed in.

"I bet she'll want to eat it because of all the mixed-up letters in it," Leon guessed. "But what about that angry elf?"

"We can use this rule to trick Fixit, too!" Violet said. "Maybe he'll like being invited to lunch. Maybe it will make him happy."

Leon shrugged. "Why not? Lunch makes me happy—if it's pizza."

Violet turned to Sprite. "You're a genius! You must have been paying attention in Royal Pixie Tricker class."

Sprite's green cheeks blushed.

"It was nothing," Sprite said. "Now, let's put this plan into action!"

8
A Tricky Invitation

After dinner, Violet and Leon made the lunch invitations. Violet made the one for Rusella. She drew flowers and butterflies all over the front. Inside, she wrote:

Dear Rusella,

Please come to a picnic lunch in my backyard on Saturday at 12:00 pm.

Meet us under the old oak tree.

Sincerely,

Violet, Sprite, and Leon

Sprite wanted to know why they couldn't have the lunch right away.

"We have to wait until Saturday," Violet explained. "We can't invite two pixies to eat with us in the school lunchroom."

"I guess not," Sprite agreed.

Leon finished up Fixit's invitation. He drew some robots on the front.

"Leon, this is a fancy picnic lunch," Violet said. "Why did you draw robots?"

"Robots are cool," Leon said. "Plus, maybe it will remind Fixit that he needs to fix mine."

Leon's robot sat up. "Hug me, Mommy!" it said. Then it sucked its metal thumb.

Violet took the invitation from Leon. "It's fine," she said. "Now, how do we deliver mail to pixies?"

"It's easy," Sprite said. He took out some pixie dust from his bag and sprinkled it on Rusella's invitation.

"To Rusella!" Sprite cried.

The invitation disappeared.

"Hey, that's cool," Leon said. "I thought that only worked to move *people* around."

"It's how pixies send mail," Sprite said. Then he sprinkled pixie dust on the other invitation.

"To Fixit!"

The second invitation vanished.

"Now what do we do?" Leon asked.

"We wait," Violet said. "And we hope that those pixies don't cause too much trouble between now and Saturday!"

9
Setting a Trap

Fixit and Rusella were busy over the next two days . . .

Fixit ruined more toys with his elf magic.
All over town, Violet saw action figures that
couldn't move. Toy trucks with square wheels.
Teddy bears that growled. There were so many
unhappy children. It was terrible!

And Rusella spread mixed-up messages all over town.

Violet's mom missed a hair appointment.

Violet's dad ordered five hundred jars of pickles for the restaurant instead of five!

Each day, Ms. Rose gave them homework. And each day, the kids in the class did the wrong homework.

The whole town was falling apart!

Violet was busy, too.

She bought a can of alphabet soup.

She talked to Sprite to find out what other food fairies like.

They made a fancy pie made of rose petals and honey, two fairy favorites.

Then Violet found pixie-sized dishes in her toy box.

"This is a sweet way to trick pixies," she told Sprite. "This fairy picnic is going to be fun!"

"Maybe," Sprite said. But he didn't sound so sure.

10
Bad Manners

On Saturday morning, Violet couldn't wait to trick the pixies.

"I hope this works," Violet told Sprite and Leon as they set up the picnic blanket. "Fixit and Rusella are out of control!"

Violet examined the blanket, pleased. It was set with normal cups, plates, and bowls for Violet and Leon. There were tiny cups and plates for Sprite, Fixit, and Rusella. Each fairy plate held a little hunk of cheese.

In the middle was the fairy pie. And a bowl of Beastie Bites breakfast cereal—Sprite's favorite human food.

Sprite licked his lips. "I haven't seen a meal this yummy since I was in the Otherworld!" he said.

"It looks like the perfect trap to me," Leon remarked.

Just then, Violet's mom walked out into the yard. She carried a crock of steaming soup.

Sprite quickly hid inside a cup.

"Here's your alphabet soup," Mrs. Briggs said.

She put the soup on the blanket. Then she ruffled Leon's hair. "I think it's so cute that you and Violet are having a little tea party."

Leon's cheeks turned red. He looked like he wanted to sink into the ground.

Violet looked at the small clock she kept in her bag of fairy tools. It was almost noon.

"Thanks, Mom," Violet said. "Uh, we need to start now."

"Of course," Mrs. Briggs said. "I'll leave you alone."

Violet and Leon waited for something to happen. They did not have to wait long.

Poof! Rusella appeared.

"Hi," Violet said, trying to sound natural. "We're just waiting for Fixit."

"Fairy rules say I have to eat lunch with you," Rusella said. "They don't say I have to wait. Let's eat!"

Rusella dove right into the food. She picked up a tiny plate and ate the hunk of cheese. Then she picked up the other plates and ate that cheese, too.

"Hey!" Sprite said.

Next, Rusella picked up the rose-petal pie. She gobbled down the whole thing.

"Wow! If I ate like that, Mom would ground me for a week," Leon whispered to Violet.

Rusella hopped next to the bowl of Beastie Bites. She popped piece after piece of cereal into her mouth.

Then Rusella burped.

"That was delicious!" she said. "And now I have to be going."

"Don't go yet!" Violet said. "You haven't had any soup."

"Great!" Rusella said. "I'm still hungry!"

Rusella rushed over to the crock of soup. She leaned in and started scooping the soup into her mouth.

"Mmmm," she said. "This is good."

Then Violet saw Rusella's smile turn to a look of horror.

"What's this?" she asked, looking at the soup in her hands. "Noodles shaped like letters? It can't be!"

"It's alphabet soup," Violet said. "We made it just for you!"

"Oh no!" Rusella stopped eating the soup. But it was too late.

A tunnel of wind appeared in the air. The swirling wind sucked Rusella into the tunnel.

"Those mixed-up letters tasted sooooo good!" Rusella yelled.

And then she disappeared.

"We did it!" Violet cried. "Sprite, look in the book."

Sprite opened up *The Book of Tricks*. A picture of Rusella began to appear on the once-blank page. Violet knew that meant that Rusella was back in the Otherworld.

Before they could celebrate, there was another *poof*!

11

Another Mix-Up!

Fixit stood on the picnic blanket.

"Okay, I'm here," said the elf. "Now, where's lunch?"

Violet frowned. There was hardly any alphabet soup left. Rusella had eaten all the cheese. And the pie. And the cereal.

"Oh, Fixit, I'm sorry," she said. "You see, Rusella was here, and—"

"That does it!" Fixit said, stomping his foot. "You invite me to lunch, and you don't even have any food?"

"Well, you were late," Leon said boldly.

"Impossible," Fixit said. "In fact, I'm early. The invitation said one o'clock."

"One o'clock?" Sprite asked, confused. "But lunch started at twelve."

"It must've been Rusella," Violet mumbled.

Fixit's face was red with rage. "I thought you children were trying to do something nice for me. To thank me for all the toys I make. Nobody ever thanks me! But this isn't nice at all. Well, I'll have my revenge. I'm going to mess up every toy in this town!"

The elf vanished in a cloud of pixie dust.

Violet thought she might cry. "We were so close!" she said. "I don't know how we're ever going to make Fixit happy. He's the most miserable creature I've ever seen."

"It's okay, Violet," Sprite said, flying in front of her face. "We did get Rusella. That makes six pixies tricked!"

"Sprite, I agree with Violet," Leon said. "I don't think there's any way to cheer up that angry elf."

Suddenly, Violet brightened. "Maybe the fairy queen can help!"

"It's worth a try," Sprite said. He took a purple stone from his bag. Queen Mab had talked to them through the stone before. She had helped them figure out how to trick Aquamarina, Bogey Bill, and Buttercup.

Violet held the stone in her hand. "Please help us," she whispered.

12

A Toy for Fixit

The stone began to glow with purple light. Then Queen Mab's face appeared in the stone. She had long pink hair, purple eyes, and brown skin.

"Hello, Violet," the queen said in her musical voice. "I understand you need help tricking Fixit."

Violet nodded, staring at the beautiful queen.

Queen Mab smiled. "To make Fixit happy, you must first find out what makes him *un*happy."

"How do we do that?" Sprite asked.

But the queen's picture faded. The stone stopped glowing.

Sprite sighed. "I'm more confused than before," he said. "This is so hard."

"Maybe not," Violet said. "The queen said we have to find out what makes Fixit unhappy. He already told us that."

"Yeah," Leon said. "He is unhappy that nobody ever thanks him for making toys."

"Right," said Violet. "So what can we do to thank him?"

"How about sending a thank-you note?" Leon suggested.

"Hmm. Maybe," Violet said.

"What if we give him a present?" asked Sprite. "I love presents!"

"That's a great idea!" Violet said. "We can make him a toy. A toy of his very own."

Violet, Leon, and Sprite got to work. Leon dug up some old wheels and boxes in his room. Violet got some paint and glitter. She found some jars of buttons, yarn, and plastic jewels that she had saved.

74

They worked all afternoon. They attached the wheels to the boxes. They strung the boxes together with yarn to make a train.

"It's beautiful, isn't it?" Violet asked when the train was done.

"It is pretty nice," Leon said.

Sprite hopped into one of the cars. "Can I go for a ride?" he asked.

"Sorry, Sprite," Violet said. "We'd better get this to Fixit. Fast."

"Right," Sprite said. "How are we going to find him?"

"Let's visit the toy store downtown," Violet suggested. "I have a feeling he's there."

Sprite sprinkled some pixie dust on them.

In a flash, they were in front of the toy shop.

"I know Fixit will be happy when he sees this," Violet said, holding up the toy train.

Suddenly, the train floated out of Violet's hands.

"No!" Violet yelled.

The train flew across the street, smashed against a wall, and crashed to the ground. It broke into pieces.

Their present for Fixit was ruined!

13
Trouble at the Toy Shop

Violet heard a familiar giggle. A cute fairy wearing purple overalls flew down from the wall.

"Spoiler!" Violet cried. "Not you again!"

Not long ago, Spoiler had tried to stop them from tricking a gremlin named Jolt.

"That broken toy should slow you down!" Spoiler cried. "By the way, Finn the Wizard says hello!" She vanished, laughing.

"Oh dear," Sprite said. "I didn't know Spoiler was working for Finn. That's very bad. Very bad indeed."

Finn, a fairy wizard, was one of the escaped pixies. He was very dangerous.

Violet picked up the broken train. "What are we going to do now?"

"We might as well make sure Fixit is here," Leon suggested. "Then we can come back tomorrow with a new present."

They walked inside the colorful toy shop. The woman behind the counter had strange, sparkly eyes.

"He must be here," Sprite whispered. "The shopkeeper is under a spell."

Violet and Leon walked down the toy aisles. They heard sounds coming from the back of the shop. They slowly walked toward the noise.

Fixit stood at a workbench, hammering square wheels onto a wooden truck. Stacked all around him were messed-up toys.

Fixit looked up from his work and scowled at them. "What are *you* doing here?"

"Well, we were trying to bring you a present," Violet began, "but then Spoiler—"

"A present?" Fixit asked. "For me?"

Violet handed him the toy train. "Sorry. It's broken," she said. "Now you'll be angrier than ever."

But Fixit looked at the train in wonder. His eyes grew wide.

"Did you—did you *make* this?" he asked.

Violet nodded.

"I helped," Leon piped up.

Fixit sat down.

"I can't believe it," he said. "I can't believe that children made me a present. A toy just for me. A beautiful, wonderful toy!"

And then Fixit did something amazing.

He smiled.

"I'm so happy!" he cried.

14
Halfway There

The wind tunnel appeared. The breeze blew the cap off Fixit's head.

Suddenly, Violet felt sorry for the elf.

"Oh, Fixit!" Violet said. "We would have made you a toy even if we didn't need to trick you. Honest!"

Fixit's smile grew wider. "I believe you!" he said as the tunnel sucked him in. "Thank youuuuuuuu!"

Fixit and the wind tunnel disappeared.

Sprite opened *The Book of Tricks*.

Violet looked at the brand-new picture of Fixit. She touched the picture.

"Good-bye, Fixit," she said. "I'll never forget you!"

Sprite made sure the shopkeeper wasn't under a spell anymore.

Then he used pixie dust to bring them all back to Violet's room.

"Okay," Violet said. "So far, we've tricked seven pixies."

"Hey, we're halfway there!" Leon said. "We only have seven more to go."

"Right," Violet said. "Sprite, what do we know about the rest of the pixies?"

"We've been looking for Hinky Pink since the beginning," Sprite said. "He's the one who can change the weather."

"And there's Spoiler," Leon said. "She causes so much trouble."

Sprite flew in a circle, like he always did when he was nervous.

"Don't forget Finn the Wizard!" Sprite said. "He worries me most of all."

Everyone was quiet for a minute.

"We shouldn't worry about Finn right now," Violet said. "There are four more pixies we don't even know about yet. Tomorrow, let's get out there and find them!"

About the Creators

Tracey West has written several book series for children, including the *New York Times*–bestselling Dragon Masters series. She is thrilled that her first series, Pixie Tricks, is being introduced to a new generation of readers.

Xavier Bonet lives in Barcelona, in a little village near the Mediterranean Sea called Sant Boi. He loves illustrating, magic, and all retro stuff. But above all, he loves spending time with his two children—they are his real inspiration.

Pixie Tricks
The Angry Elf

Questions and Activities

Rusella messes up messages. She admits that she changed the date on Brittany's party invitation. What other messages does she mess up?

When Fixit appears in Leon's bedroom, he messes with Leon's toy robot. What does he do to it and why?

Why do you think Violet feels sorry for Fixit in the end? Reread pages 84–85.

Sprite, Violet, and Leon prepare a picnic lunch for Fixit and Rusella. The foods include rose-petals-and-honey pie, cheese, and alphabet soup. What other foods do you think pixies might like?

The Pixie Trickers build a toy train for Fixit! What toy would *you* build for him? Draw it and label its parts.